The Wandering Smurf

Random House
New York

First American Edition. Based on original story by Yvan Delporte. This translation Copyright © 1981 by Peyo. License of SEPP Brussels. All rights reserved under International and Pan-American Copyright Conventions. Published in the United States by Random House, Inc., New York, and simultaneously in Canada by Random House of Canada Limited, Toronto. Originally published in different form in Great Britain by Stafford Pemberton Publishing, Ltd., Cheshire. Copyright © 1980 by Peyo SEPP. Library of Congress Catalog Card Number: 81-50253 ISBN: 0-394-84931-0

Manufactured in the United States of America

7 8 9 0

SMURF is a trademark of SEPP International S.A.

Life was jolly and pleasant in Smurfland. There was laughing and singing all day long. But one Smurf was not happy at all. He stood by his hut, sad and lonely.

The other Smurfs tried everything to cheer him up. Out-of-tune Smurf played his guitar. Baker Smurf offered him one of his best cakes. And Joker Smurf gave him a funny present. But nothing could cheer up the sad Smurf.

He was sad because there was only one thing he wanted to do. He wanted to travel. He dreamed of wandering around the world to faraway places and strange countries. Smurfland was nice, he thought, but the grass had to be greener somewhere else.

One day he woke up and said, "Today I am leaving Smurfland!" He tied his few things in a big red handker-chief. Now he was ready to start out to see the big, wide world.

Papa Smurf was sorry to see him go. But he wanted the sad Smurf to be happy, so he said, ''Have a nice trip. And take this magic whistle. If you are ever in any danger, just blow the whistle and you'll be safe.''

Wandering Smurf said good-bye to all his Smurf friends. Then he marched out of the village. At last he was going to travel! He would have great adventures. He would cross deserts. He would climb mountains. He would sail the vast oceans!

After walking all day, Wandering Smurf grew tired. As the sun was setting in the west, he entered a big forest. It's getting dark, he thought. I'll find a nice place to sleep under those big trees.

He found a small clearing carpeted with soft moss. He gathered a few blades of grass for a bed. Now he was ready to spend his first night away from home. He felt sure he would dream of ex-citing adventures.

But the forest was filled with strange noises. There was creaking…and bumping…and screeching. Wandering Smurf was scared. He couldn't sleep a wink.

Wandering Smurf didn't see the owl that was perched on the branch of a nearby tree. The owl, as hoot owls will do, called, "WHOOOO! WHOOOO!"

The eerie "WHOOO! WHOOO!" startled Wandering Smurf.

What...what is that! Could it be an evil spirit searching for a Smurf? he wondered.

Wandering Smurf was frightened. <u>Very</u> frightened! How could he fight the evil spirit?

Suddenly he remembered the whistle from Papa Smurf. Perhaps it could chase evil spirits away!

I will blow the whistle, Wandering Smurf decided. It is my only hope!

So Wandering Smurf put
the whistle to his lips and
blew as hard as he could.
There was a loud BANG, a
flash of light, a gust of wind,
and a cloud of dust!
What was happening?

All of a sudden, Wandering Smurf was back in Smurfland! The magic whistle had brought him back home. Papa Smurf and all the other Smurfs were so happy to see him.

And do you know what? Wandering Smurf was very happy, too.

That night, the Smurfs had a big party with cakes and music and dancing. Wandering Smurf ate and sang and danced.

But he knew that some-day he would wander out again to see the big, wide world.